Phonics Friends

Zack's Zippers
The Sound of **Z**

The Child's World

By Cecilia Minden and Joanne Meier

The Child's World

Published in the United States of America
by The Child's World®
PO Box 326
Chanhassen, MN 55317-0326
800-599-READ
www.childsworld.com

*A special thank you to Stan Koenig for being such a
perfect "Zack."*

The Child's World®: Mary Berendes, Publishing Director

Editorial Directions, Inc.: E. Russell Primm, Editorial
Director and Project Editor; Katie Marsico, Associate
Editor; Judith Shiffer, Associate Editor and School Media
Specialist; Linda S. Koutris, Photo Researcher and
Selector

The Design Lab: Kathleen Petelinsek, Design and Page
Production

Photographs ©: Photo setting and photography by Romie
and Alice Flanagan/Flanagan Publishing Services: cover,
4, 6, 8, 10, 12, 14, 16, 18; Corbis/Gallo Images/Peter
Lillie: 20.

Library of Congress Cataloging-in-Publication Data
Minden, Cecilia.
   Zack's zippers : the sound of Z / by Cecilia Minden
and Joanne Meier.
      p. cm. — (Phonics friends)
   Summary: Simple text featuring the sound of the letter
"z" describes what Zack finds in his zippered pockets.
   ISBN 1-59296-311-0 (library bound : alk. paper)
[1. English language—Phonetics. 2. Reading.] I. Meier,
Joanne D. II. Title. III. Series.
   PZ7.M6539Zac 2004
   [E]—dc22   2004003546

Note to parents and educators:
*The Child's World® has created Phonics Friends with
the goal of exposing children to engaging stories and
pictures that assist in phonics development. The books
in the series will help children learn the relationships
between the letters of written language and the indi-
vidual sounds of spoken language. This contact helps
children learn to use these relationships to read and
write words.*

*The books in this series follow a similar format.
An introductory page, to be read by an adult, intro-
duces the child to the phonics feature, or sound, that
will be highlighted in the book. Read this page to the
child, stressing the phonic feature. Help the student
learn how to form the sound with her mouth. The
Phonics Friends story and engaging photographs follow
the introduction. At the end of the story, word lists
categorize the feature words into their phonic element.
Additional information on using these lists is on The
Child's World® Web site listed at the top of this page.*

*Each book in this series has been carefully written
to meet specific readability requirements. Close atten-
tion has been paid to elements such as word count,
sentence length, and vocabulary. Readability formulas
measure the ease with which the text can be read and
understood. Each Phonics Friends book has been ana-
lyzed using the Spache readability formula. For more
information on this formula, as well as the levels for
each of the books in this series please visit The Child's
World® Web site.*

*Reading research suggests that systematic phonics
instruction can greatly improve students' word recogni-
tion, spelling, and comprehension skills. The Phonics
Friends series assists in the teaching of phonics by
providing students with important opportunities to
apply their knowledge of phonics as they read words,
sentences, and text.*

This is the letter *z*.

In this book, you will read words that have the *z* sound as in:

zipper, zebra, and *zoo.*

This is Zack.

Zack likes zippers.

Zack likes big zippers.

Zack's coat has a big zipper.

Zack likes little zippers.

Zack's pocket has a little zipper.

Zack looks in his pocket.

What is in Zack's pocket?

There is a toy zebra.

Zack looks in his other pocket.

What is in the pocket?

There is a ticket in Zack's pocket.

It is a ticket to the zoo!

"I hope I see a real zebra

at the zoo," says Zack.

Fun Facts

Did you know there are three kinds of zebras living in Africa? Africa is the only continent where you can find zebras living in the wild. Not all zebras look exactly alike. Some may have slightly different coloring or stripe patterns. Zebras always travel together in herds. One male zebra called a stallion, several mothers, and their young make up a family herd. Until young male zebras can create their own family herds, they travel in herds with other young males.

The Berlin Zoo in Berlin, Germany, the Bronx Zoo in New York City, New York, and the San Diego Zoo in San Diego, California, are the world's largest zoos. Many people consider the Vienna Zoo in Vienna, Austria, to be the world's oldest zoo. It opened in 1752. There are approximately 1,500 zoos worldwide.

Activity

Learning the Different Ways Zippers Are Used

Look around your home to discover all the ways zippers are used. Of course, you will check the coat closet. Don't forget to look in the laundry room. Maybe there is a laundry bag with a zipper on it. Check all over the house and make a list. Have your family guess how many different ways zippers are used in your home. You will probably surprise them when you share your list.

To Learn More

Books
About the Sound of Z
Flanagan, Alice K. *Zigzag: The Sound of Z.* Chanhassen, Minn.: The Child's
    World, 2004.

About Zebras
Fontes, Justine, and Ron Fontes. *How the Zebra Got Its Stripes.* New York:
    Golden Books, 2002.
Macken, JoAnn Early. *Zebras.* Milwaukee: Weekly Reader Early Learning, 2002.
Reitano, John, and William Haines. *What If The Zebras Lost Their Stripes?* New
    York: Paulist Press, 1998.

About Zippers
Butterfield, Moira, and Peter Utton et al. *Zippers, Buttons, and Bows.* Hauppauge,
    N.Y.: Barron's Educational Series, 2000.
Pulver, Robin, and R. W. Alley. *Mrs. Toggle's Zipper.* New York: Four Winds Press,
    1990.

About Zoos
Geisel, Theodor (Dr. Seuss). *If I Ran The Zoo.* New York: Random House, 1950.
Jolivet, Joelle. *Zoo-ology.* Brookfield, Conn.: Roaring Brook Press, 2003.

Web Sites
Visit our home page for lots of links about the Sound of Z:
    http://www.childsworld.com/links.html

Note to Parents, Teachers, and Librarians: We routinely check our Web links to make sure
they're safe, active sites—so encourage your readers to check them out!

Z Feature Words

Proper Name
Zack

**Feature Words in
Initial Position**
zebra
zipper
zoo

About the Authors

Cecilia Minden, PhD, directs the Language and Literacy Program at the Harvard Graduate School of Education. She is a reading specialist with classroom and administrative experience in grades K–12. She earned her PhD in reading education from the University of Virginia. Cecilia and her husband Dave Cupp enjoy sharing their love of reading with their granddaughter Chelsea.

Joanne Meier, PhD, has worked as an elementary school teacher and university professor. She earned her BA in early childhood education from the University of South Carolina, and her MEd and PhD in education from the University of Virginia. She currently works as a literacy consultant for schools and private organizations. Joanne Meier lives with her husband Eric, and spends most of her time chasing her two daughters, Kella and Erin, and her two cats, Sam and Gilly, in Charlottesville, Virginia.